DACHSHUNDS

Valerie Bodden

Creative Education · Creative Paperbacks

published by Creative Education and Creative Paperbacks
P.O. Box 227, Mankato, Minnesota 56002
Creative Education and Creative Paperbacks are imprints of
The Creative Company
www.thecreativecompany.us

design and production by Christine Vanderbeek
art direction by Rita Marshall
printed in the United States of America

photographs by Alamy (Collection Christophel, Entertainment
Pictures), Dreamstime (Julius Elias), Getty Images (Rudolf
Vlcek), iStockphoto (baratroli, falcatraz, rusm, utkaman-
darinka), Shutterstock (Utekhina Anna, Owen Brown,
Ysbrand Cosijn, dogboxstudio, In Green, Eric Isselee,
Kalmatsuy, Csanad Kiss, Jakub Krechowicz, Liliya
Kulianionak, Erik Lam, Petr Lerch, leungchopan, Neveshkin
Nikolay, otsphoto, Scorpp, Viorel Sima, SmileStudio,
Nikolai Tsvetkov, WilleeCole Photography)

library of congress cataloging-in-publication data
Names: Bodden, Valerie, author.
Title: Dachshunds / Valerie Bodden.
Series: Fetch!
Includes bibliographic references and index.
Summary: A brief overview of the physical characteristics,
personality traits, and habits of the dachshund breed, as
well as descriptions of famous pop-culture dachshunds
such as Buster.
Identifiers:
ISBN 978-1-60818-899-4 (hardcover)
ISBN 978-1-62832-515-7 (pbk)
ISBN 978-1-56660-951-7 (eBook)
This title has been submitted for CIP processing under
LCCN 2017938925.
CCSS: RI.1.1, 2, 4, 5, 6, 7; RI.2.1, 2, 5, 6, 7;
RI.3.1, 5, 7; RF.1.1, 3, 4; RF.2.3, 4

first edition HC 9 8 7 6 5 4 3 2 1
first edition PBK 9 8 7 6 5 4 3 2 1

TABLE OF CONTENTS

Funny Dachshunds **5**

What Do Dachshunds Look Like? **6**

Dachshund Puppies **10**

Dachshunds on the Screen **13**

Dachshunds and People **14**

What Do Dachshunds Like to Do? **18**

A Famous Dachshund **23**

Glossary **24** • Read More **24** • Websites **24** • Index **24**

FUNNY DACHSHUNDS

A dachshund (*DAHKS-hund*) is a **breed** of dog.

Dachshunds are funny dogs that love to play.

They are smart and loving, too. Sometimes

dachshunds can be stubborn.

WHAT DO DACHSHUNDS LOOK LIKE?

Dachshunds are long dogs with short legs. They look like hot dogs. Some people call them wiener dogs. Dachshunds have long *muzzles* and long ears.

Dachshunds' long ears fly up when they run fast.

There are two sizes of dachshunds. Standard dachshunds are about 10 inches (25.4 cm) tall. They weigh 16 to 32 pounds (7.3–14.5 kg). Miniature dachshunds are even smaller. Dachshunds can have short or long fur. The fur can be a mix of red, brown, black, or tan.

DACHSHUND PUPPIES

Newborn dachshund puppies weigh less than one pound (0.5 kg). But the puppies grow quickly. Soon they begin to run around. Dachshund puppies are fun to watch. They can be clumsy!

Dachshund puppies should spend lots of time with people and other dogs.

DACHSHUNDS ON THE SCREEN

Dachshunds have been in many cartoons and movies. In Walt Disney cartoons, Dinah the Dachshund is Pluto's girlfriend. Buddy is a dachshund in the 2016 movie *The Secret Life of Pets*. He joins with other pets to help rescue two dogs named Max and Duke.

Buddy (left) enjoys massages from the kitchen stand mixer.

DACHSHUNDS AND PEOPLE

The name *dachshund* means "**badger dog.**" About 400 years ago, hunters in Germany used dachshunds to hunt badgers. They hunted other small animals, too. Today, some dachshunds still hunt. Others are **show dogs**.

Longhaired dachshunds tend to be quieter and calmer than those with short fur.

Fetch!

Dachshunds make good pets. They are good with the kids in their own family. But they may snap at strangers. Standard dachshunds are less nervous than miniature dachshunds. Standards can be easier to train, too.

With a deep bark, alert dachshunds are good guard dogs.

Fetch!

WHAT DO DACHSHUNDS LIKE TO DO?

Most dachshunds need to live inside. If they are kept outside, they might bark or dig. Dachshunds need exercise every day. They like short walks and outdoor games.

Dachshunds prefer to play inside when it is wet or cold.

Fetch!

Dachshunds love to use their noses! You can hide your dachshund's favorite toy. Then, let him sniff it out. You will both have a lot of fun!

A FAMOUS DACHSHUND

Buster is a dachshund in the 1999 Walt Disney movie *Toy Story 2*. The dog is friends with the toys in the movie. One of his favorite games is sniffing out Woody the cowboy. Buster lets the toys ride on his back. He is also friends with Slinky Dog. Slinky is a toy dachshund with a stretchy body. An older Buster appears in *Toy Story 3* (2010).

GLOSSARY

badger an animal with short legs and long claws that lives in holes in the ground

breed a kind of an animal with certain traits, such as long ears or a good nose

muzzles the nose and mouth of some animals, such as dogs

show dogs dogs that compete in dog shows, where judges decide which dogs are the best examples of each breed

READ MORE

Heos, Bridget. *Do You Really Want a Dog?* North Mankato, Minn.: Amicus, 2014.

Johnson, Jinny. *Dachshund*. North Mankato, Minn.: Smart Apple Media, 2015.

Schuh, Mari. *Dachshunds*. Minneapolis: Bellwether Media, 2016.

WEBSITES

American Kennel Club: Dachshund
http://www.akc.org/dog-breeds/dachshund/
Learn more about dachshunds, and check out lots of dachshund pictures.

Bailey's Responsible Dog Owner's Coloring Book
http://classic.akc.org/pdfs/public_education/coloring_book.pdf
Print out pictures to color, and learn more about caring for a pet dog.

Every effort has been made to ensure that these sites are suitable for children, that they have educational value, and that they contain no inappropriate material. However, because of the nature of the Internet, it is impossible to guarantee that these sites will remain active indefinitely or that their contents will not be altered.

INDEX

bodies 6, 9
Buster 23
cartoons and movies 13, 23
exercise 18
fur 9
hunting 14
miniature dachshunds 9, 17
playing 5, 18, 21
puppies 10
sizes 9, 10
show dogs 14
standard dachshunds 9, 17